Space

WHEN?

WHEN WAS THE SUN BORN?

Om KIDZ
An imprint of Om Books International

WHEN?

CONTENTS

- When was the Sun born? — 3
- When does night fall in the middle of the day? — 3
- When do I call the moon a 'New Moon'? — 4
- When did man first walk on the Moon? — 4
- When does Mercury complete a day? — 5
- When can I see Mercury in the sky? — 5
- When was the first visit made to Venus? — 6
- When does Venus complete its year? — 6
- When did the first robot Rover go to Mars? — 7
- When were craters formed on Mars? — 7
- When was the 'Great Red Spot' first noticed on Jupiter? — 8
- When will Juno reach Jupiter? — 8
- When were Saturn's rings discovered? — 9
- When do auroras occur on Saturn? — 9
- When does the Sun shine on Uranus's poles? — 10
- When did we come to know about Miranda? — 10
- When did Neptune complete its first orbit after its discovery? — 11
- When did Voyager 2 track the 'Great Dark Spot'? — 11
- When can I see the Orionids? — 12
- When will Halley's Comet return? — 12
- When did the first rocket enter space? — 13
- When did the first man go to space? — 13
- When did the first woman travel to space? — 14
- When was the first artificial satellite sent to space? — 14
- When did Rosetta first land on Comet 67P? — 15
- When was Hubble Space Telescope sent into space? — 15

Find out!

Does the Sun really rise and set everyday?

WHEN?

1. When was the Sun born?

The Sun was born five billion years ago. It was formed from a giant, rotating cloud of gas and dust known as the solar nebula. The nebula collapsed, spun faster and flattened into a disk. Most of the material was pulled toward the centre and the Sun was born.

Pocket fact

Every second, the Sun releases about one million times more energy than everyone on Earth uses in one year!

2. When does night fall in the middle of the day?

This happens during a solar eclipse. A solar eclipse occurs when the Moon comes between the Sun and Earth. The Moon casts a shadow on Earth's surface and blocks out the Sun's light. So, for a few seconds or minutes, it appears as if the day has turned into night.

Find out!
Compare the size of Earth and Moon. If Earth were a basketball of 10 inches, what would the size of Moon be?

3 When do I call the Moon a 'New Moon'?

The Moon is called New Moon when it is not visible from Earth. On a New Moon day, the Moon is aligned between Earth and Sun. It is so close to the Sun that we cannot see the Moon. Besides, on a New Moon day, the Moon rises when the Sun rises and sets with it.

4 When did man first walk on the Moon?

Pocket fact
The Moon is the fifth largest satellite in our solar system. It circles the Earth at a speed of 6,000 kmph!

Astronauts from US flew on a spacecraft Apollo II, and landed on the Moon on 20 July 1969. Neil Armstrong and Buzz Aldrin were the first men to walk on the Moon. They climbed onto the dusty surface and drove around in a moon buggy. They also put the US flag to show that they had visited the Moon.

Find out!

What are the names of spacecrafts that have visited Mercury till now? When were they sent there?

WHEN?

5 When does Mercury complete a day?

Mercury is the planet closest to the Sun. It spins on its axis very slowly, but orbits the Sun faster than the other planets. A day on Mercury is equal to 59 Earth days! On the other hand, it completes a year in just 88 Earth days.

6 When can I see Mercury in the sky?

Pocket fact

Mercury has a very thin atmosphere. It is a combination of oxygen, sodium, hydrogen, helium, and potassium. Atoms that were blasted off the surface by the solar winds create Mercury's exosphere. This makes breathing difficult on Mercury.

Mercury is very hard to spot. You can only see Mercury when it is closest to the Sun. Mercury's rotation on its orbit takes it close to the Sun 13 times in a century! During this time you can see it as a black dot crossing the Sun. This is called transit of Mercury. The transit of Mercury was seen on 11 November 2019 and will be seen again on 13 November 2032. Remember to watch out for Mercury on that date!

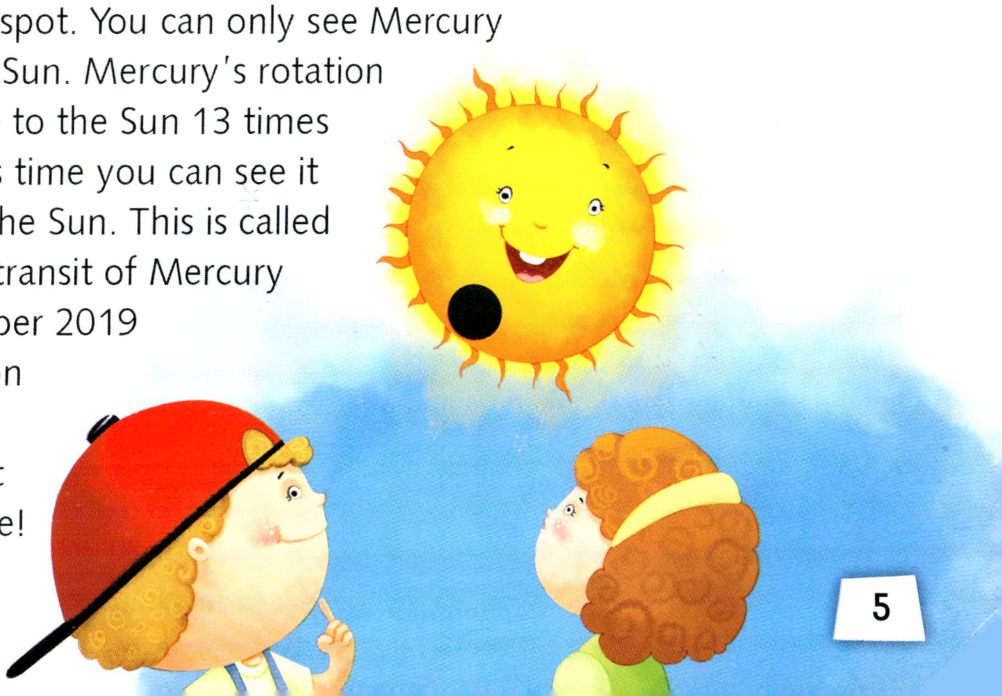

> **Find out!**
> Venus is referred to as 'Earth's twin'. Why?

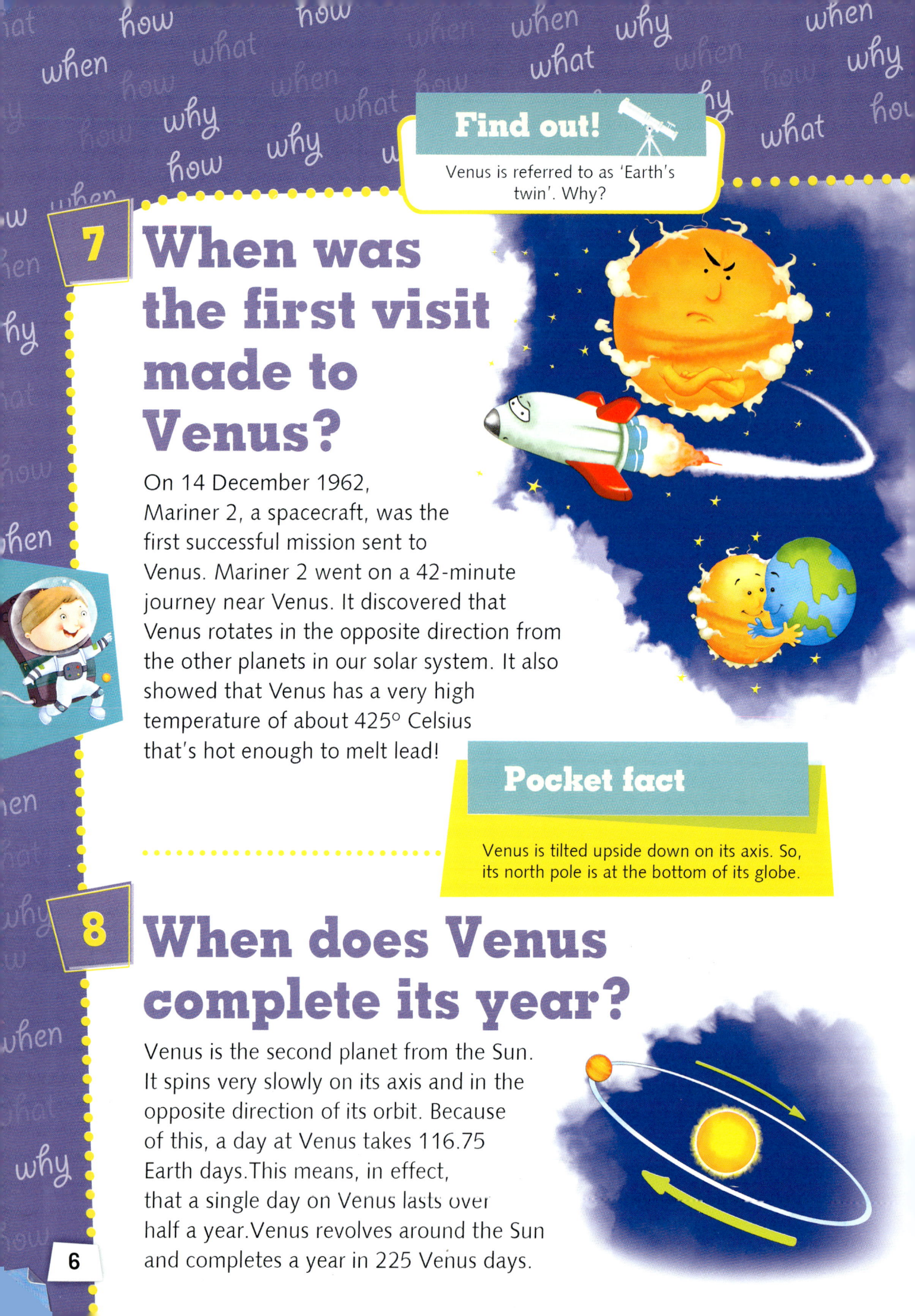

7 When was the first visit made to Venus?

On 14 December 1962, Mariner 2, a spacecraft, was the first successful mission sent to Venus. Mariner 2 went on a 42-minute journey near Venus. It discovered that Venus rotates in the opposite direction from the other planets in our solar system. It also showed that Venus has a very high temperature of about 425° Celsius that's hot enough to melt lead!

> **Pocket fact**
> Venus is tilted upside down on its axis. So, its north pole is at the bottom of its globe.

8 When does Venus complete its year?

Venus is the second planet from the Sun. It spins very slowly on its axis and in the opposite direction of its orbit. Because of this, a day at Venus takes 116.75 Earth days. This means, in effect, that a single day on Venus lasts over half a year. Venus revolves around the Sun and completes a year in 225 Venus days.

Find out!

Why is Mars red in colour?

WHEN?

9 When did the first robot Rover go to Mars?

Mars Pathfinder's Sojourner Rover was the first robot to land on Mars on 6 July 1997. Rover was a six-wheeled vehicle. Rover was sent to gather information about the soil and rocks on Mars. It was controlled from Earth by an operator. As Mars is distant from Earth, commands sent to the Rover from Earth took about 10 minutes to reach it!

Pocket fact

You could jump three times higher on Mars than you can on Earth. This is because Mars has a weaker gravitational force than Earth.

10 When were craters formed on Mars?

A crater is formed when there is an explosion. Mars has many craters on its surface. These were formed by meteorite impacts more than 3.8 billion years ago. The Bonneville Crater is a large crater, around 689 feet (210 metre) wide.

7

Find out!
How many moons does Jupiter have? Do you know the names of all of them?

11 When was the 'Great Red Spot' first noticed on Jupiter?

The 'Great Red Spot' is actually a giant storm on Jupiter. It was first noticed in 1664 by Robert Hooke. It is more than twice the size of our planet! The 'Great Red Spot' is a massive hurricane that spins counter clockwise. It spins once in six days.

Pocket fact
Jupiter is the largest and heaviest planet in our solar system. It weighs around 2.5 times more than the weight of all the other planets put together!

12 When will Juno reach Jupiter?

Juno is a NASA spacecraft which will help scientists know more about the planet Jupiter. It was launched on 5 August 2011, and reached Jupiter in July 2016. Juno's current mission is to probe beneath Jupiter's cloud cover and discover its true nature.

Find out!

What are Saturn's rings made of?

WHEN?

13 When were Saturn's rings discovered?

Saturn is the sixth planet from the Sun in our solar system. It is known for its rings that make it the fifth brightest object in space. The rings of Saturn were first discovered by astronomer Galileo in 1610.

Pocket fact

Saturn is very light. If placed in water, it could just float on it.

14 When do auroras occur on Saturn?

Sometimes dazzling light shows called auroras appear on Saturn's north and south poles. Auroras occur when particles from the Sun get drawn towards Saturn's atmosphere. These auroras are large and bright and can continue shining for days.

Find out!

Why does Uranus appear blue in colour?

15 When does the Sun shine on Uranus's poles?

Sun shines on the north and south poles of the planet Uranus for nearly a quarter of a year! Each year on Uranus is equal to 84 Earth years. The Sun shines directly over each pole for about 21 Earth years, while the other half of the planet has a long, dark winter.

Pocket fact

While most planets spin on their axis, like a top, Uranus rotates on its side like a rolling ball! The planet is tipped over because of a major collision with a celestial object.

16 When did we come to know about Miranda?

Miranda is one of the 27 moons of Uranus. It was discovered on 16 February 1948 by planetary astronomer Gerard Kuiper.

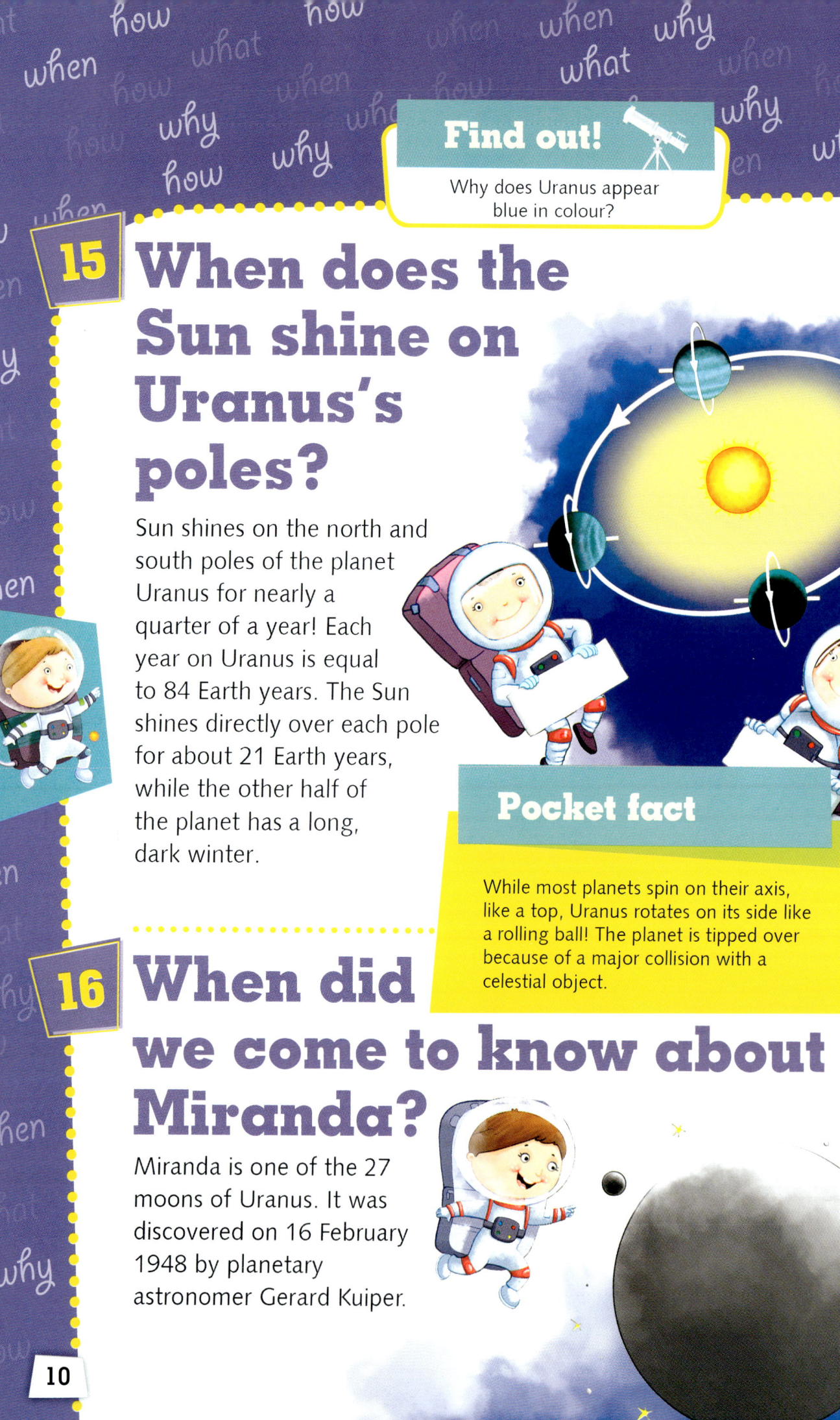

Find out!
Which is the only spacecraft to have visited Neptune? In which year did it go there?

WHEN?

17 When did Neptune complete its first orbit after its discovery?

Neptune is the eighth planet in the solar system. It is at a distance of 4.5 billion kilometres from the Sun. Neptune was discovered in 1846. It completed its first orbit around the Sun in 2011 after a period of 165 Earth years.

Pocket fact
Neptune was the first planet located using mathematical predictions by a French mathematician, Urbain Le Verrier, rather than through regular observations of the sky.

18 When did Voyager 2 track the 'Great Dark Spot'?

The spacecraft, Voyager 2, tracked a large, oval-shaped, dark storm in Neptune's southern hemisphere. This was called the 'Great Dark Spot'. It was large enough to contain the entire Earth! It spun counterclockwise, and moved westward at almost 1,200 kilometres an hour.

11

Find out!

How is a meteor different from a meteorite?

19 When can I see the Orionids?

The Orionid meteor shower is one of the two meteor showers from Halley's Comet. Orionids are very active during 20 and 21 October of every year. At its peak, you can see around 20 meteors every hour!

Pocket fact

Hartley 2 is a peanut-shaped comet. It orbits the Sun every 6.46 years. The spacecraft, Deep Impact, flew close to this comet in November 2010.

20 When will Halley's Comet return?

It will return in the year 2062. Halley's Comet orbits the Sun every 75-76 years, so this is the year when it will appear in the sky and will be seen from Earth. Halley's Comet was recorded by Edmund Halley in 1682. It was seen again in 1758, 1835, 1910, and 1986.

Find out!
What is a gyroscope?

WHEN?

21 When did the first rocket enter space?

The first rocket was launched into space in 1942. It was named the V2 rocket. It was developed by Wernher Von Braun, a German. The V2 had gyroscopes that could steer the rocket to a specific location.

Pocket fact

The farthest an astronaut has travelled from Earth is 401,056 kilometres, by Jim Lovell, Jack Swigert, and Fred Haise, aboard Apollo 13.

22 When did the first man travel to space?

On 12 April 1961, Russian cosmonaut, Yuri Gagarin, became the first man to travel into space. He launched into orbit on the Vostok 3KA-3 spacecraft (Vostok 1). Vostok 1 travelled around Earth once every 108 minutes. It reached a maximum height of 327 kilometres.

Find out!
Name some of the satellites in space.

23 When did the first woman travel to space?

Valentina Tereshkova, a Soviet Union (now Russia) cosmonaut was the first woman to go to space. She went on a three-day journey to the space aboard the spacecraft Vostok 6 in June 1963.

Pocket fact
Animals flew into space before humans! Laika, a stray dog was the first animal to be sent to space in November 1957.

24 When was the first artificial satellite sent to space?

The world's first artificial satellite was Sputnik 1. It was sent into orbit by the Soviet Union on 4 October 1957. Sputnik 1 was a metal ball with four radio aerials sticking out of it. It orbited Earth for 22 days before its batteries ran out!

Find out!

Have we sent any spacecraft to Pluto?

WHEN?

25 When did Rosetta first land on Comet 67P?

Rosetta, a spacecraft, is on a 10-year mission to catch a comet and land a probe on it. It was launched in 2004, and reached Comet 67P on 6 August 2014.

26 When was Hubble Space Telescope sent into space?

Pocket fact

Luna 2 (Lunik 2), the Soviet Union spacecraft, was the first man-made object to reach another world. It crashed into Moon on 14 September 1959.

The Hubble Space Telescope is a telescope and camera that observes space. It was placed in a low Earth orbit by the space shuttle Discovery in April 1990. It is operated by a remote control from Earth.

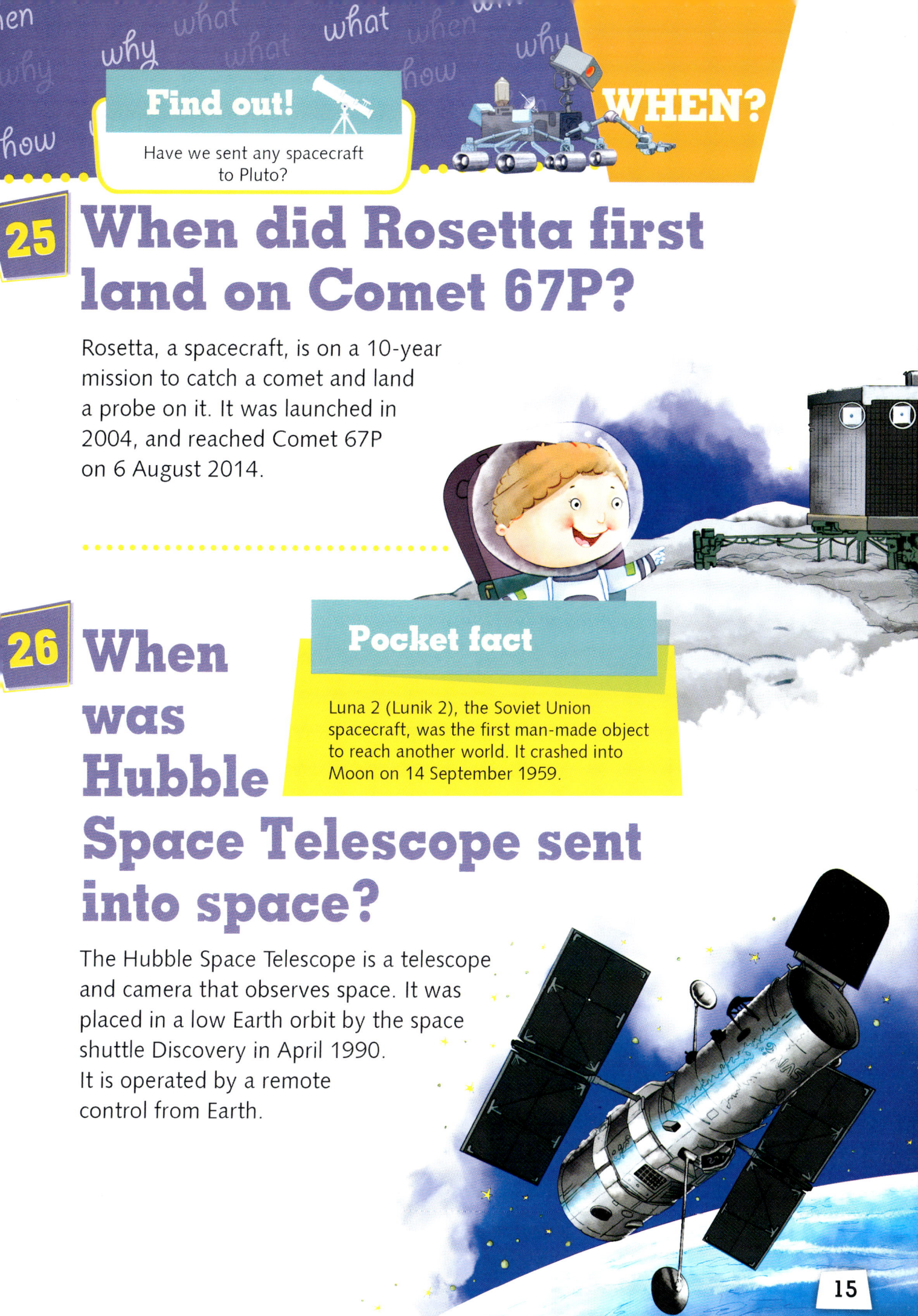

OTHER TITLES IN THIS SERIES

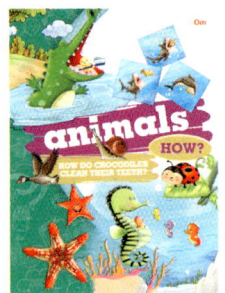   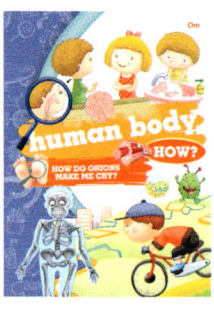  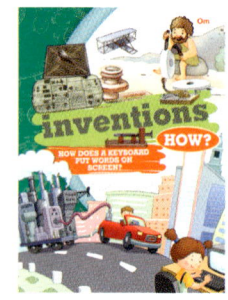
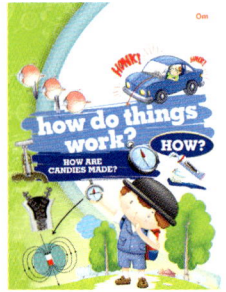  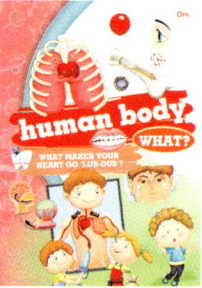  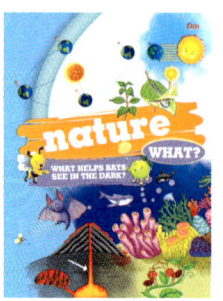 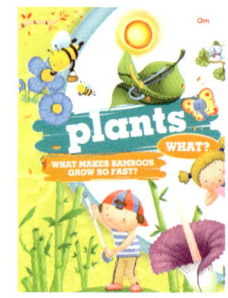
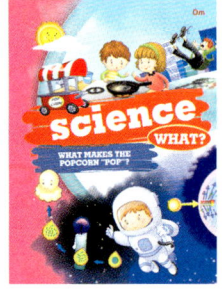 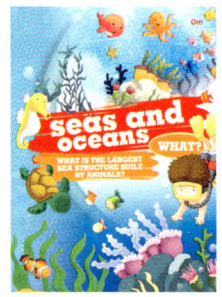   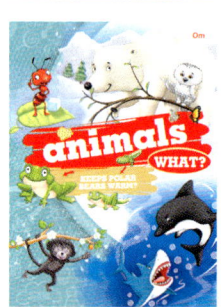 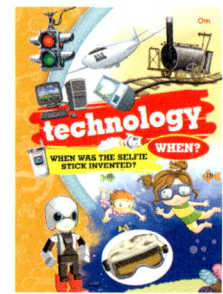
 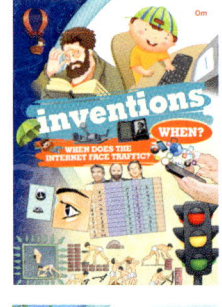 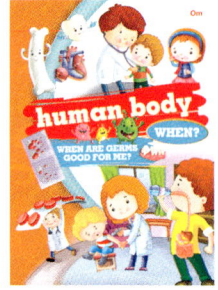 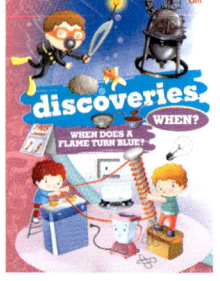 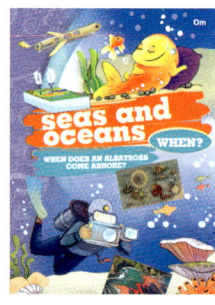 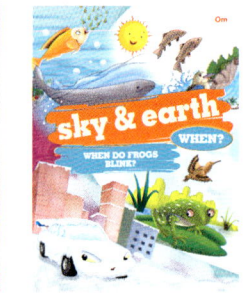
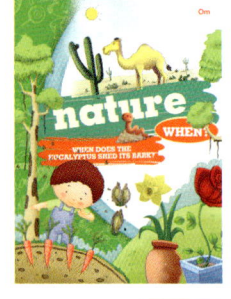 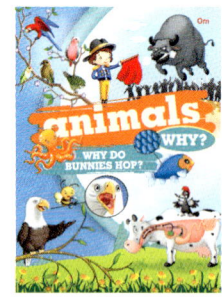 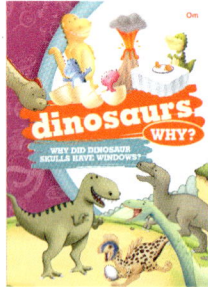  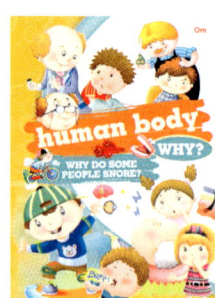 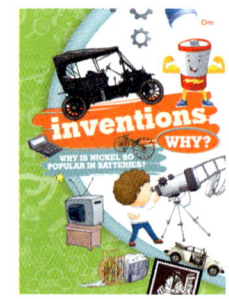
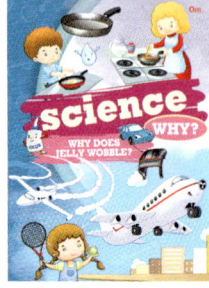 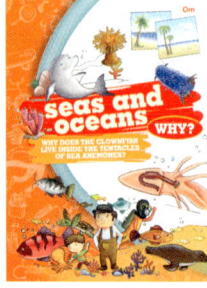   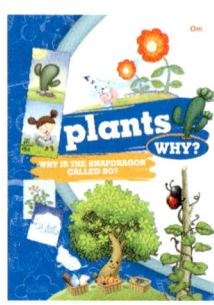